# WHEN THE BIG DOG BARKS

BY
## MUNZEE CURTIS

PICTURES BY
## SUSAN AVISHAI

GREENWILLOW BOOKS
NEW YORK

Text copyright © 1997 by Munzee Curtis
Illustrations copyright © 1997 by Susan Avishai. All rights reserved. No part of this
book may be reproduced or utilized in any form or by any means, electronic or
mechanical, including photocopying, recording, or by any information storage and
retrieval system, without permission in writing from the Publisher, Greenwillow Books,
a division of William Morrow & Company, Inc., 1350 Avenue of the Americas,
New York, NY 10019.

Printed in Hong Kong by South China Printing Company (1988) Ltd.
First Edition   10  9  8  7  6  5  4  3  2  1

LIBRARY OF CONGRESS CATALOGING-IN-PUBLICATION DATA
Curtis, Munzee.
When the big dog barks / by Munzee Curtis; pictures by Susan Avishai.
p.    cm.
Summary: A child knows that her parents will always be
there to protect her when she is afraid or at risk.
ISBN 0-688-09539-9 (trade).    ISBN 0-688-09540-2 (lib. bdg.)
[1. Fear—Fiction.    2. Parent and child—Fiction.]    I. Avishai, Susan, ill.
II. Title.    PZ7.C2677Whb    1997    [E]—dc20    96-10412    CIP    AC

For my father, with love
—M. C.

For Buzzy
—S. A.

If I climb too high
on the monkey bars,
Papa saves me.

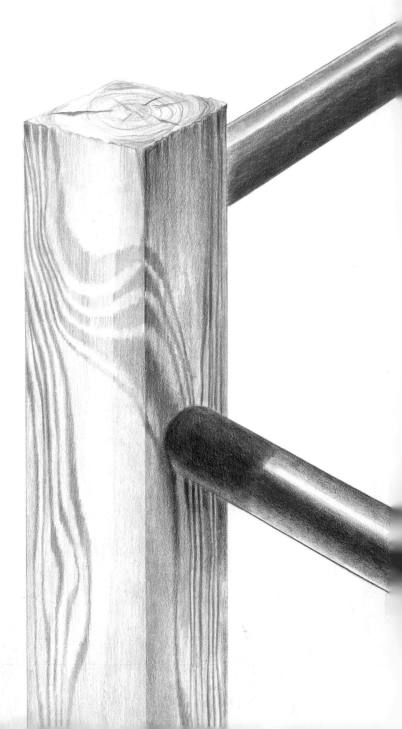

When a stranger says,
"And what's your name?"
Mama lets me hide
behind her.

On a stormy night
when thunder comes,
Papa holds me.

When the little dog licks me,
Mama helps me pet him.

When the big dog barks,
Papa holds my hand
until we get past him.

When the babysitter comes
and Mama goes out,
Mama always comes back.

When I watch the witch
in "The Wizard of Oz,"
Papa sits close by.

When someone wants
my favorite doll,
Mama says I don't
always have to share.

When I go to bed,
they leave the night light on.
And when I call,
they come.

"We'll keep you safe,"
my mama says.

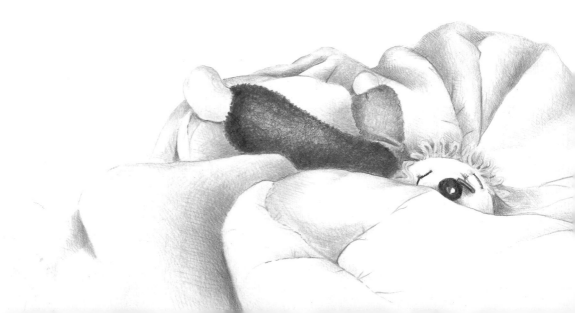

And I know they do.